Peace, Love, and K-POP

By Precious McKenzie

Illustrated by Becka Moore

ROURKE
Educational Media
rourkeeducationalmedia.com

www.rourkeeducationalmedia.com

Edited by: Keli Sipperley
Cover and Interior layout by: Tara Raymo
Cover and Interior Illustrations by: Becka Moore

Library of Congress PCN Data

Peace, Love, and K-Pop / Precious McKenzie
(Rourke's World Adventure Chapter Books)
ISBN (hard cover)(alk. paper) 978-1-63430-392-7
ISBN (soft cover) 978-1-63430-492-4
ISBN (e-Book) 978-1-63430-586-0
Library of Congress Control Number: 2015933787

Printed in the United States of America,
North Mankato, Minnesota

Dear Parents and Teachers:

Rourke's Adventure Chapter Books engage readers immediately by grabbing their attention with exciting plots and adventurous characters.

Our Adventure Chapter Books offer longer, more complex sentences and chapters. With minimal illustrations, readers must rely on the descriptive text to understand the setting, characters, and plot of the book. Each book contains several detailed episodes all centered on a single plot that will challenge the reader.

Each adventure book dives into a country. Readers are not only invited to tag along for the adventure but will encounter the most memorable monuments and places, culture, and history. As the characters venture throughout the country, they address topics of family, friendship, and growing up in a way that the reader can relate to.

Whether readers are reading the books independently or you are reading with them, engaging with them after they have read the book is still important. We've included several activities at the end of each book to make this both fun and educational.

Are you ready for this adventure?

Enjoy,
Rourke Educational Media

Table of Contents

Chapter One

Arrested

"What do you mean? We have to wait here for a lawyer?" Aunt Bernadette frantically cried at the military police officer. "We're United States citizens. Don't we have rights?"

The officer gave Aunt Bernadette a cold, emotionless stare and turned to walk out of the room. He opened the door, then turned back toward us and hissed, "You are not in the United States anymore. You will follow our laws."

The heavy steel door slammed shut behind him. Aunt Bernadette paced the room like a panther in a cage. Tomas sat in a chair in the corner, his knees tucked up to his chin. His arms wrapped around his legs and his head rested on his knees. I knew he wished we were anywhere but a North Korean military station. I sat motionless in the opposite corner of the room.

It was our fault we were here, not Aunt Bernadette's. I felt horrible, especially since we were having a great visit to South Korea until this happened. Now we might never make it back home to the US. We'd broken the law and crossed from the democratic republic of South Korea into communist North Korea. Even worse, if we ever saw Mom and Dad again, they'd probably ground us forever.

"Marisol, stop crying," Aunt Bernadette snapped at me. "It won't make anything better." I didn't realize I was crying but tears were streaming down my face.

"I'm sorry," I blubbered, wiping my face with the back of my hand.

Tomas raised his head, worry spread across his round twelve-year-old face. I walked over and put my arms around him. As his twin, sometimes I could sense exactly what he was feeling. Aunt Bernadette still paced the room.

"Mari, what will happen to us? Will we see Mom and Dad again?"

"I hope so, Tomi, I hope so."

"It's all my fault, you know," he said.

I shook my head. "It's my fault too."

Yes, it was his idea to go canoeing in the river inlet. But I did jump in the canoe with him because I was bored. Dad was busy doing research in a museum archive as part of his job as a history professor. Mom had gone out for a while, shopping for groceries. We were tired of sitting around. We wanted to explore Korea more. There were four canoes just sitting in the park. Why not, we thought?

What Tomas and I didn't expect was the force of the river current. We paddled as hard as we could but we drifted farther from the South Korea shore. Before we knew it, we'd crossed the border and were in North Korean territory. When Aunt Bernadette realized how far we'd drifted, she panicked. She grabbed a canoe and paddled out to bring us back to South Korea. But, like us, the current pulled her across the border too swiftly.

Before Aunt Bernadette could even see if Tomas and I were okay, a North Korean military officer had his machine gun pointed in Aunt Bernadette's back. We were quickly handcuffed and led away from the river.

Although we'd been traveling around Korea for three weeks, we hadn't really learned about the demilitarized zone. Until today.

"Did you know they'd arrest us?" I whispered to Aunt Bernadette. I looked around the room for hidden video cameras.

She stopped pacing and knelt down beside me.

"Or shoot you two. That's why I came after you," she said.

She explained the tense history between North and South Korea. "At the end of World War II, to keep Japan out of Korea, Russia and the United States split Korea down the 38th Parallel. Russia would control the north, the United States would control the south."

She took a shaky breath and continued. "Russia made North Korea a communist government. The US made South Korea a democracy. Korea hasn't been united since. Both sides stockpile weapons and never take their eyes off each other. No trust. No friendship." Aunt Bernadette rubbed her eyes. She looked tired, hopeless.

"After the Korean War, in 1953, the 150-mile-long demilitarized zone between north and south was created to keep the tension and the fighting down," she said.

"A no-man's land," Tomas whispered.

"You got it. But you can see all the soldiers on either side, always ready to fight," Aunt Bernadette shook her head. "I don't get it. It is time for peace."

I managed a half smile. Aunt Bernadette was our hippie, peace-loving aunt. Her favorite song was John Lennon's Give Peace a Chance.

"What will they do with us?" I asked.

"I don't know. We can only stay calm and wait," she said.

Chapter Two

Volcano

Until we got arrested in North Korea, our first three weeks in South Korea were phenomenal. We spent our first couple of days relaxing on Jeju Island, just off the coast. Mom said Jeju Island is a favorite honeymoon spot for newlyweds. I could see why; it is beautiful. There's a volcano, forests, and waterfalls. Koreans say that Jeju Island is the garden of the gods, cultivated on Earth.

Mom's a bird biologist so she was totally thrilled about Jeju Island. She decided that our first stop on the island should be Hallasan National Park, to hike up the volcano. Dad's not really the athletic type, although he tries. The volcano would be hard for him to climb but he wasn't going to be left behind. Aunt Bernadette is all healthy with her organic foods and morning yoga, so nature is her thing. Tomas and I agreed it would be awesome to see a real volcano up close too. Back home in Chicago we have a lot of things but there's no volcano.

The hike would take us all day. Dad filled a backpack with plenty of water bottles, snacks, and a first-aid kit. Tomas and I started out at a jog, excited to reach the top.

"Slow down, kids, save your energy," Dad called out to us.

We laughed and waved as we ran away. The grownups could catch up to us at the top of the mountain. It was only six miles to the top.

"Do you think it will erupt today?" Tomas asked excitedly. I think he was secretly hoping for an eruption so he could see the red hot lava spilling down its sides.

"Nope," I huffed as I ran. "It's been dormant for years."

Tomas looked a little disappointed so I added, "Who knows? I guess it could still blow at any time."

That thought kept his interest.

Tomas followed close at my heels as we ascended the mountain. Roe deer bolted through the forest, probably surprised by two noisy kids. About ten minutes into our adventure, Tomas started to whine.

"Marisol, slow down, I'm tired. I've got a cramp." He grabbed his side and doubled over.

"But we have at least five more miles to go," I said.

Tomas dropped to the ground. " I need a water break."

I waited as patiently as I could, tapping my foot on the ground as he drank from his water bottle.

"Jeez, settle down," he said. "Give me a minute."

After that, Tomas never regained his speed. We moved slowly but steadily up the mountain, stopping to take pictures with our cell phone. Mom, Dad, and Aunt Bernadette must have been moving even slower. We didn't see them.

We followed the trail higher and higher until it looked like we could touch the clouds.

"Are we there yet?" Tomas groaned.

"Almost to the top," I said happily. We'd been hiking up the mountain for three hours. We had to be getting close to the summit.

Forty-five minutes later, we reached the top of the volcano. Other tourists lounged around the benches, snapping photos, drinking water, and relaxing after a four-hour hike.

"Tomi!" I shouted, "Look down! There's the crater!" It was huge and it looked like a lake. Tomas didn't respond, he just grabbed my cell phone and started snapping photos.

We stood by the railing, completely amazed at the size of the volcano.

"Can you believe we made it to the top?" I asked him.

"Nope. I had no idea I could hike for four hours," he joked.

"Looks like we'll have to wait for Mom, Dad, and Aunt Bernadette." I was in no hurry to descend the mountain. It would take us at least three hours to reach the bottom.

We sat on a bench for what seemed like an eternity until Aunt Bernadette, Dad, and Mom reached the summit.

"What took you so long?" Tomas yelled.

"Respect us old people," Dad said. "We move a little slower than you young people."

With her eyes turned toward the sky, Mom said, "Look at the clouds moving in. A storm is coming. We better head down the mountain. Don't want to get caught up here in bad weather." She was right. Thick dark clouds were blowing in. Hallasan Mountain was known for its quickly changing weather. We wasted no time heading down the mountain.

The wind picked up speed. I thought the hike down would be easy. I was wrong. After the four hour climb up the mountain, my legs felt like rubber. It was hard to walk.

Rain soon pelted us from all sides. The wind whipped the rain around us. "Take shelter," Mom shouted, "This storm might last a while." We looked around for a shelter but found none.

"We'll use nature instead," Mom said. She led us off the trail and into the forest.

"Use this canopy of leaves, it will block some of the storm," she said. Together, the five of us huddled under the canopy of leaves, shivering in the cold rain.

"I always imagined volcanoes as hot," I said almost sarcastically.

"Well, you should see this place in winter. Covered in snow," Dad said. "I saw photos in the visitor's station."

Lightning lit up the sky. "Let's sit on the ground," Mom suggested. "We don't need to be lightning rods."

For another hour, the rainstorm blew across the mountain. By the time it was over, we were drenched and freezing cold.

Aunt Bernadette looked sad. I soon understood why. She had spotted a sign when we got back on the trail. She studied the map on the sign. "We've got about two and a half hours to walk if we want to make it to the bottom of the mountain. It's going to be a long walk down."

"Carry on, troops," Dad tried to sound cheerful but he too was wet, tired, and cold.

The rest of the hike was miserable. Tomas was grouchy because he was hungry and his candy bar stash got ruined when Dad accidentally sat on the backpack while we waited out the rainstorm. Our feet hurt and our legs were wobbly and weak.

By the time we reached the bottom of the volcano, I felt delirious. We'd hiked more than seven hours! Up and down hills. I pointed this out to Aunt Bernadette and she perked up.

"What a workout! Think of the calories we burned!" It seemed like that thought alone made all of our suffering worth it for Aunt Bernadette. "Cheer up, crew! We did it! We conquered a volcano!"

Dad smiled at his optimistic big sister. He rubbed his sore, blistered feet. "We did. And I think we deserve a nice, big dinner when we get back to our hotel."

"Yippee!" Tomas said and did a happy dance around Dad. I swear that boy only thinks about his stomach.

Chapter Three

Busan

We left Jeju Island and headed up Korea's east coast to its second largest city, Busan. For his research, Dad needed to visit two ancient temples there.

I thought Busan was fun. It is a busy, modern city with great beaches. During our first day in Busan, Mom and Aunt Bernadette took us on a harbor tour. Dad stayed at the hotel, preparing his notebooks for the next day's research. Since our trip to Mexico, when he got horribly seasick on a whale watching tour, Dad stays far away from boats.

The boat cruised through Busan's harbor. The sun set and we saw the twinkling lights of the high rise buildings along the shore.

"It looks like stars," Aunt Bernadette said to me as we stood near the ship's railing.

"I didn't expect this in Korea," I said.

She gave me a puzzled look. "What do you mean?"

"I guess I expected ancient pagodas and rice fields," I confessed.

"Oh Marisol, you watch too many American movies," she said. "Korea is a major, industrial nation. It is not stuck in the past."

The ship moved across the waves.

"Look, the Gwangan Bridge," Aunt Bernadette pointed to a long bridge that arched across the harbor.

Tomas popped up behind us. "Looks like Christmas lights on the bridge except it's not Christmas."

"Beautiful," Mom said as she met us on the deck. "Are you having fun?"

Almost in unison, Tomas and I said yes.

"Good, good. Tomorrow we'll go to the Beomeosa Temple with your father." Mom looked relaxed and happy on the water.

The four of us stood on deck, quietly watching the lights from the city.

Dad didn't let us sleep in the next morning.

Right after breakfast, we took the subway to the Beomeosa Temple. It was built about 1,300 years ago. To get to the temple, we had to climb another mountain.

"We're certainly getting our exercise in Korea," Aunt Bernadette said proudly.

Tomas gave her an annoyed look. He wasn't much of a fitness fanatic.

We walked up step after step, winding our way up the mountain to the temple. At the top, from the temple, we could see the entire city of Busan. The high rise buildings looked like tiny models, not mega buildings.

"Well kids, I've got a meeting with a monk. See you in a couple hours." Dad smiled and slapped Tomas's back. Obviously, a meeting with a monk was something to get excited about.

"What shall we look at?" Mom asked us.

Tomas held up a brochure. "Let's find the well with the gold water."

"There's no such thing as gold water," I said.

"This brochure says there is." He stuck his tongue out at me.

"Let's go find out," Mom said. She put an arm

around each of us and led us into the temple.

Aunt Bernadette snapped pictures of the pagoda and the pillars.

Buddhists prayed in the temple. Mom reminded us to be quiet and respectful because it is a place of worship.

We found a large koi pond in a courtyard.

"I found goldfish but not gold water," I said.

Mom scanned the brochure. "The name Beomeosa means Nirvana Fish Temple," she said.

"Cool, we're in a fish temple," Tomas said.

Aunt Bernadette said, "Listen to this, Tomas. There's a legend that claims that on this spot, golden fish came down from heaven on a five-colored cloud."

Careful not to disturb the people who were praying, we walked between the buildings, admiring the colors and shapes.

When we walked around the corner of the temple, we saw Dad in combat with a man in a robe. I could see the sweat on Dad's face. The man kicked at Dad. Dad jumped back, then fell on his back. The man kicked again. Dad rolled away, narrowly escaping the man's foot. Dad leapt up.

The man lunged at Dad, twirling his leg. Kick. Kick. Kick. Dad fell forward, his face scraped in the dirt.

"Alberto!" Mom cried as she rushed to help Dad escape from the crazed attacker. Aunt Bernadette grabbed her arm, and pulled her back.

"Stop, Carolina, you'll get yourself killed," Aunt Bernadette barked at Mom. "Mari, hold your mother."

Aunt Bernadette yanked Mom's hand and placed it in mine.

Aunt Bernadette rushed to Dad's side. She took a martial arts pose. Her face looked like steel.

Then she shouted, and sprang on the attacker, slicing through the air with her hands and feet. The attacker backed away, narrowly jumping out of her reach.

Aunt Bernadette looked like a tiger as she fought off the man. The attacker finally stopped, held up his hands, and said, "Enough. Enough."

The man bent over, sweaty, and laughed, "I'll get you next time Alberto."

Aunt Bernadette looked from the man to Dad. "What? You know him?"

Dad sat on the ground laughing, "Of course,

this is Chin-Hwa. He is a Buddhist monk."

We were still confused.

"He lives here," Dad said. "He was showing me the tactics of the ancient fighting monks."

Chin-Hwa stepped forward. "It is lovely to meet you. Welcome to Korea."

We shook his hand.

"Fighting monks? I didn't know monks were supposed to fight," Tomas said, his eyes wide.

I whispered to Mom, "I didn't know Aunt Bernadette could fight."

Chin-Hwa smiled at Tomas. "We did. We do. It is an ancient and secret art form. Our monks used these skills to chase the Japanese out of our temple hundreds of years ago. Your father, the astute historian, wanted a hands-on historical demonstration."

"Looks like I'm not as fast on my feet as Aunt Bernadette is," Dad said.

"A single lady has to know how to take care of herself. I can fight if I need to," Aunt Bernadette said.

Chapter Four

Fresh Fish

"I heard there's an amazing fish market nearby," Aunt Bernadette said. "Who wants to go for lunch?"

"I do!" Tomas yelled.

We hopped on the subway to make our way to the Jagalchi Fish Market.

Inside the building were rows of light bulbs hovering over rows of water-filled tubs. Small, dark haired women wore rubber gloves and talked with customers.

Every tub was filled with sea creatures.

Tomas was very excited. He loved fish.

"Mari, look, there's sea cucumbers!" He pointed to another tub. "Shrimp!" Then another tub. "Sea squirts! Fish! Spool worms! They are all alive!"

"Yeah," I replied, "Like a very weird aquarium."

"It is so awesome!" He acted like he was at a petting zoo.

Aunt Bernadette, Mom, and Dad walked ahead of us.

We soon caught up with them. They had stopped at a stall and were pointing at fish and handing money to the woman.

"Hey, Dad's buying us a pet fish. It looks like a perch," Tomas said happily.

"Uh, Tomi, I hate to tell you," I started to say, but then a loud chopping sound destroyed Tomas's hopes of a pet fish.

Tomas's face wrinkled up, tears sprang into his eyes. The woman handed Dad a plate full of chopped fish and rice.

"What just happened?" Tomas stuttered.

"Dinner!" Aunt Bernadette sang.

Tomas looked at me. "This is a food market?"

"Uh, yeah," I answered. "Not a pet store."

"But, but, but, they're all alive," he stammered.

"Fresh," Dad said.

"Fresh," Tomas whispered.

"Straight from the ocean to the table," Aunt Bernadette added.

The adults gathered around a small table, chopsticks in their hands.

Tomas was still processing what happened. "Dad took the fish out of the tub. The woman took it. Chopped it up and put it on a plate."

"Um-hmm," Dad mumbled as he chewed.

"She didn't even cook it," Tomas said.

"Nope, it's raw like sushi," Mom said.

Tomas couldn't clear the shock from his mind.

"Sit down and eat kids, before it's all gone." Dad patted the empty seats beside him, rice stuck to his face.

I didn't see anything wrong with fresh fish. I ate sushi in Chicago. I dug in. It was delicious. With each bite I took, and the longer I chewed, the sweeter and more buttery the fish tasted. Tomas looked like he was ill.

"No thanks." He pushed the chopsticks away and held his stomach.

"Suit yourself, kiddo. It's a long time until dinner," Dad said.

Chapter Five

Busan Tower

Tomas moaned. "I feel dizzy. And I think I'm going to be sick."

"Go find the bathroom," I barked at him.

We were at the top of the Busan Tower, over 400 feet high in the sky. Heights usually made Tomas feel ill. From the tower we could see the entire city of Busan, even the harbor with passenger ferries and container ships.

"Come with me. I don't want to go by myself," he whined.

"Don't be a baby. Go," I ordered him. Really, sometimes Tomas could be so immature. He sighed and stumbled away, searching for the bathroom.

Mom and Dad were looking through binoculars to see the city. Aunt Bernadette was talking to a Korean man by the stairwell, pointing to a map.

Tomas was taking forever in the bathroom. If

he would have eaten lunch at the fish market like the rest of us, he probably wouldn't have felt so sick.

When he walked out of the bathroom, I asked, "Feeling better?"

He nodded. "Yes, but something weird happened in there."

"What?" I asked.

"Well, this guy walked in and three other guys in dark suits and sunglasses came in behind him."

"Go on," I said.

"When the guy goes to the toilet, the other three guys hover around right outside the door. Then they follow the guy out the door. Didn't you see them?"

To be honest, Busan Tower was busy. People were crowded around enjoying the view. I didn't pay attention to who went in and out of the bathroom. Tomas seemed worried.

"What if they are criminals?" Tomas asked.

"Did they bother you?"

"No, but I felt uncomfortable," Tomas said.

"Forget about it. They're probably long gone by now," I said.

We walked around the tower for a short time. Then our parents decided we should go back to the hotel to rest before dinner.

Outside the tower, a camera crew positioned themselves behind metal gates, to keep the crowd out.

"What's going on?" Mom asked a tour guide.

"They are filming a music video," he answered.

"Tomi, let's get a closer peek," I whispered. "Follow me."

I took his hand and slid between people until we had a clear view of the set.

"Looks like a K-Pop star," I said.

"That's the guy I saw in the bathroom," Tomas said.

Korean girls next to us giggled hysterically and screamed. Dancing in front of us was one of Korea's biggest K-Pop stars, TaeYang. He was stylish, charming, and singing his heart out for the cameras.

"There's the other guys," Tomas said and pointed to the left. There were three larger men in dark suits and sunglasses standing close by.

"I bet those are TaeYang's bodyguards," I said. Tomas nodded.

"His music isn't bad," Tomas remarked. "It's kind of catchy."

"I don't have a clue what he's singing about," I said. It was true. All the K-Pop lyrics were in Korean.

TaeYang danced closer to the crowd. He winked at the girls. He reached out his hand. The girls next to me almost clawed him to pieces. I tried to step back from the chaos. Then TaeYang's hand reached out for mine. Before I realized it, he had pulled me onto his dance floor. The cameras were filming, music blasting from the speakers. TaeYang grooved around me, serenading me with his pop song.

"Dance, Mari," Tomas shouted above the crowd.

I tried to forget about all the people watching me dance. I tried to relax and move to the bubbly Korean pop beat. TaeYang smiled and nodded at me. I must be doing okay, I thought. So I kept dancing. He circled around me as he sang, holding my hand and staring into my eyes. When his song ended, TaeYang leaned closer to me and gave me a kiss on the cheek. The crowd went wild, screaming at TaeYang. All of the girls wanted him to kiss them, too.

The bodyguards led me away from TaeYang. He waved to the crowd then hopped into a limo.

"WOW," Tomas said. "You just danced with a pop star!"

"He was kind of cute," I admitted.

"Maybe you'll be in his new video. You'll be famous!"

"I doubt it," I said, laughing.

"I wonder what he was singing about?"

"I'm guessing it was a love song."

It was kind of fun being serenaded by a pop star. Not to sound cheesy, but I felt like royalty. I just didn't want Tomas to know how much I liked it because if he found out, he'd tease me about it forever.

Chapter Six

Pop Star

The next day was full of surprises. During breakfast at our hotel, Mom's cell phone rang.

"Hello, Mrs. Perez?" I heard a woman's voice through the speaker.

"Yes," Mom said.

"Yes, huh, hello, this is Mee-Yon. I am a director with K-Pop, a TV show in Korea. We have video of your daughter dancing with TaeYang near Busan Tower. We'd like to know if she, and your family, would like to be guests on our show."

Mom raised her eyebrows at me. "Yes, yes, of course. We'd love to come."

Mom jotted down the television studio's address. We finished up breakfast then got ready to head to the studio.

As we rode the subway, Tomas twitched and wiggled in his seat.

"Sit still," I said to him.

"I can't. I'm so excited. We get to be on a TV show! We'll be stars!" He bounced out of his seat.

"We're not stars. We're just special guests," Mom corrected Tomas.

Even though Mom pretended not to be excited, I knew she was. Before we left the hotel, she made all of us shower, brush our teeth, comb our hair, and put on our best outfits. She said she wanted us to look "respectable."

Aunt Bernadette chimed in, "Well, I'm excited about the TV show. I love K-pop music. It is so fun, so techno, so good for dancing."

Dad rolled his eyes. "It's just like American pop music. Good to dance to but no real, serious message in it."

Dad listened to music with messages like save the world and give peace a chance. You get the idea.

We rode the subway for another twenty minutes to the TV studio. Once inside, we were dazzled. With the lights, the cameras, and crew members running from stage to stage, it was busy! Make-up artists powdered men and women, painted on lipstick, and dusted on blush. Nervous singers sang warm-up chords to prepare their voices for the show. Audience members started to pour through the doors and take their seats around the stage.

"This is the Korean American Idol," Tomas whispered.

Mee-Yon met us. She gave us special passes to wear clipped to our shirts. Then she told us to sit in a row of seats close to the stage. We could almost reach out and touch the pop stars on the stage.

"This is so cool," I said to Tomas.

Tomas nodded. Even Dad looked like he was having fun. Soon, an all-girl band came to the stage. The crowd screamed.

The girls danced around the stage, singing in Korean. They wore mini-skirts, knee-high boots, and tight T-shirts, like American pop stars. They smiled at the crowd and bounced around as the audience applauded.

When they left the stage, another group came on. This time it was an all-boy band. They wore black leather and had spikey hair. They sang as they danced, crooning to the girls in the audience.

"I wish I knew what they're singing about," Dad remarked.

"Does it matter? It's fun!" Aunt Bernadette screamed and clapped for the performers.

A roar came up from the crowd. I looked around to see why the audience was going so wild. TaeYang strode across the stage, waving and smiling to the audience.

TaeYang opened his set with a rock song, electric guitars and techno keyboards backing him up. The song almost sounded angry. His next song was completely different. It was slow, soft, and sounded romantic. In the middle of the song, the spotlight landed on my face. TaeYang walked slowly across the stage, right to me.

He held out his hand. I reached out and he pulled me up onto the stage. He held my hand and led me around the stage, smiling and singing. Girls threw flowers at the stage. He picked up a rose and gave it to me. I think I blushed a little.

At the end of the song, he leaned over and gave me a kiss on the cheek. Then he led me backstage. I could hear the fans screaming at the top of their

lungs. TaeYang must be big news in Korea. Why did he want to dance with me? A total stranger?

"Thank you for coming tonight," TaeYang said sweetly.

"You're welcome," I stammered. He was kind of cute.

"You are not from Korea?" he asked.

I shook my head, "No, Chicago," I answered.

"Are you a K-Pop fan?"

"I didn't know what K-Pop was until yesterday."

TaeYang laughed. "Is it better than American Pop?"

"A little," I admitted.

TaeYang laughed again.

My family burst backstage, rushing up to me and TaeYang.

"Mari, that was so awesome!" Tomas gushed.

Mee-Yon introduced my family to TaeYang.

Dad cleared his throat. "Can I ask a question?"

Mee-Yon and TaeYang looked at Dad.

"Why did you go to all this trouble? Why did you invite us to the show?"

Mee-Yon said, "After the crowd saw your daughter dancing with TaeYang at Busan Tower yesterday, all the social media sites went wild for the tall, dark-haired girl." She pointed to me. "The fans think she's pretty."

Mee-Yon paused for a minute. "We wanted your daughter to come back so more people could see her and help TaeYang top the charts with his new love song. Maybe she could go out to dinner with him? Be seen together?"

A-ha! TaeYang was releasing his brand new love song. By pulling a strange, new, unknown girl onto the stage, he could really make his audience curious. It was a publicity stunt.

Mom turned to Mee-Yon. "Thank you, Mee-Yon, and thank you Mr. TaeYang. That is very kind of you." Mom smiled politely. "But my daughter is only twelve years old. She's too young to date a K-Pop star."

"Twelve?" TaeYang stuttered. "But she is so tall."

Aunt Bernadette laughed. "And athletic. She looks older." Aunt Bernadette patted my shoulder.

TaeYang and Mee-Yon looked embarrassed, like they'd made a horrible mistake.

"Please don't be offended," TaeYang said.

"I'm not," I said. "It was fun to dance with a K-Pop star."

"Thank you," TaeYang said. "To make it up to your family, please, please stay at my apartment in Seoul."

Dad shook his head. "No, we couldn't do that."

Mee-Yon said, "Then let us pay for your —"

Mom interrupted Mee-Yon. "No, no. Please, don't worry about it. We had such a fun time watching the filming of the TV show. It was no trouble."

Mee-Yon and TaeYang really thought that somehow they'd made Mom and Dad angry. They weren't. They thought it was kind of silly. I was flattered that the fans thought I was cute. Besides, it was fun to be on stage, dancing with a real star.

"Let us take you out to a real Korean dinner," Mee-Yon suggested.

Never someone to turn down free food, Dad said, "Yes!"

We rode in a limo to a Korean restaurant called An Ga that served Korean barbeque. We dug into bowls full of delicious meat and sauces, sharing our food family style. I was getting better at using chopsticks. Poor Tomas kept dropping the meat. Eating with chopsticks really made Tomas slow down between bites, mostly because he dropped so much food.

Mee-Yon told us more about K-pop and its stars. Korean pop music is big business, like American pop music. "I guess we're not so different. We all love music that makes us feel like dancing."

Tomas became TaeYang's biggest fan. He downloaded all of TaeYang's music, learned the words—in Korean—and even learned how to dance like TaeYang. He watched the video of me dancing with TaeYang over and over again.

"Just wait until we get back to Chicago! Our friends will never believe you were on stage, on TV, with a K-Pop star," Tomas said. "Or, that we went out to dinner with a star!"

"Yeah, nobody in Chicago knows who TaeYang is. It's no big deal," I said.

Okay, maybe it was a big deal, dancing with Korea's biggest K-Pop star, but who am I to brag about it?

Chapter Seven

Seoul

Dad needed to get to Seoul so he could begin teaching a history class at Seoul National University. We set off on the train to Korea's largest city, Seoul. There were ancient Buddhist temples right next door to huge, modern skyscrapers. Dad said that after the Korean War, Seoul was crumbling and poor. Today, Seoul sparkles. With more than 10 million people, Seoul is full of movement and action.

We dropped Dad off at the university. Mom kissed his cheek and said, "Go teach those young people!"

"Where are we going?" Aunt Bernadette asked after Dad walked away. She looked ready for adventure.

"Food!" Tomas shouted.

"I know just the place," Aunt Bernadette said.

We rode the subway to the Insadong, a neighborhood in Seoul. Aunt Bernadette was right. Food was everywhere! Tiny restaurants, tea houses, and food carts lined the streets. The air smelled like pastries and roasting meat.

I could practically see Tomas's mouth watering. "Where should we eat first?" he asked.

"Now, now, little man. You don't need a bellyache," Aunt Bernadette said. "Let's choose one restaurant for today. We can shop the rest of the afternoon."

We agreed on a small stand that served Korean barbeque. After our dinner with Mee-Yon and TaeYang, Tomas was hooked on Korean barbeque. It was his favorite food. Then we strolled the streets, wandering through the alleyways, looking for good deals on Korean souvenirs. I found socks

with small Korean children sewn on them and Korea stitched across the toes. Aunt Bernadette found a Korean flag.

"Kids, we should head back to the university. Dad said they would have our apartment ready this evening," Mom said.

Because Dad was teaching for the university, they gave guest teachers an apartment to live in while they were in Korea. We wouldn't have to spend two months in a hotel room.

When we met Dad at the university, he had the apartment keys and a map. "Ready to see our new place?"

We hopped on the subway, ready to find and move into our new Korean home.

"It will probably be small," Dad warned us as we walked to the apartment complex. Space is expensive in a big city. We knew that from living in Chicago. When Dad typed in our security code and threw open the front door, we were totally shocked.

"Oh my." Aunt Bernadette sighed. "Where will I sleep?"

"Alberto," Mom said quietly, "this can't be right for all five of us."

Dad gave us a weak smile. "Maybe it isn't that bad."

Our living room had a small sofa, a TV on the wall, and a closet system. The kitchen was right there, too, not even separated by a wall.

"Where do we cook?" Tomas asked as he turned in circles in the narrow kitchen area. Our refrigerator was only as tall as Tomas. A microwave oven sat on top of the refrigerator. Two cook top burners and a small sink were all we had for a kitchen. With no dishwasher, we'd have to wash everything by hand.

"This is going to take some getting used to," Mom said.

Our bathroom was even smaller than the kitchen. The toilet and sink were right next to the shower. When we'd shower everything in the bathroom would get soaking wet.

"We can make it work, Carolina," Dad said, trying to cheer up Mom.

Aunt Bernadette wasn't convinced either. "Let's see the bedroom."

The bedroom had one large bed and a sofa. That was all. So that meant three of us had a place to sleep.

"Marisol, shall you and I camp out on the living room floor?" Aunt Bernadette asked.

"Looks like we have too," I said.

For the first night, we used the sofa cushions as pillows and slept in our clothes. But the next day, we found a department store and bought real pillows and two sleeping bags.

Showering was tough too. With one bathroom to share between five people, we weren't allowed to stay in the bathroom all day, doing our hair and putting on makeup. We agreed to do that stuff in the kitchen so everyone had time to shower in the mornings.

"Why are apartments so small in Korea?" Tomas whined one morning.

"Where are you going to put ten million people?" Mom said. "Homes must be small."

Chapter Eight

Olympic History

On Dad's day off from teaching, we headed for the Olympic Park. Dad remembered watching the 1988 Olympic Games from Seoul on TV when he was a boy. He wanted to visit the Olympic Park and Museum to see it all for himself.

When the Olympic Games were in Seoul, Korea wanted the world to know how important harmony and peace were to them. For the Olympics, Korea had a World Peace Gate built. The World Peace Gate looks modern but also has ancient Korean features and images of ancient Korean gods. We walked around the gate, looking up at the Korean art.

"Mari, look, a tiger!" Tomas pointed to one of the animals on the World Peace Gate. "And a dragon, a bird, and a snake!"

I took pictures with my cell phone. In the center

of the gate, the large Torch of Peace burned. Dad decided to give us a history lesson.

"You see, kids," Dad said, "South Korea wanted the world to see them as an ancient culture. But they also wanted the world to see them as a rising, powerful nation in Asia."

Tomas and I nodded even though we were more interested in the animals on the gate. Dad started talking about North Korea, and Tomas and I, only half-listening, walked away to look at the rest of Olympic Park.

We met up with Aunt Bernadette by the water. She watched water fountains shoot high into the air.

"Looks like the water is dancing," she said to us.

"Aunt Bernadette, can we follow the walking paths?" Tomas asked, pointing to a winding sidewalk.

"Of course, sweetie. You know I love my exercise," she said.

Mom and Dad stayed near the water fountain while Aunt Bernadette went with me and Tomas on the walking paths. We walked for a while near the water.

"It is so peaceful here," Aunt Bernadette said as we walked. "You would never know we are in the middle of the city."

"Will the Olympics come to Seoul again?" Tomas asked.

Aunt Bernadette thought for a moment. "Probably not. They try to find new cities for the Olympics so one country doesn't look like the favorite."

I told Tomas, "Korea made this Olympic spot a park for everyone to enjoy and use."

Tomas liked that idea. "It's nice to have lots of parks in a big city. People need places to relax." Sometimes my twin brother surprised me. He could be kind of smart.

After our walk on the trail, Aunt Bernadette insisted we visit the SOMA, or Seoul Olympics Museum of Art. We could always benefit from culture, she said.

As soon as we walked inside the museum, I knew it was different than other museums I've visited. Bright colored art, funky sculptures, and video surrounded us.

"Awesome!" Tomas said.

"It is modern art," Aunt Bernadette told us. "Let's explore!"

Mom and Dad went one way in the museum. Aunt Bernadette stayed with us until she found a huge human sculpture.

Tomas tugged at my arm. "Come on, let's go without her. She's so slow."

We wandered around a few rooms, taking in the wild modern art on the walls.

"Buckets, Mari!" Tomas practically shouted. "The roof must be leaking."

Three blue buckets were in a circle in the center of the room. Water dripped from the ceiling into the buckets.

"For such a fancy museum, they need to fix their roof," Tomas said.

As Tomas walked around the buckets, he tripped and kicked one bucket over. Water sloshed across the floor.

"Oh, way to go," I said to him. "Go find a paper towel and clean it up."

As he turned around to walk away, he knocked over the second bucket and then the third.

"You're graceful," I said to tease him. "Now you need a mop."

A security officer blew his whistle and ran over to us. He angrily waved his hands and pointed at the floor and at the buckets.

"Yes, sir, sorry, sir," Tomas stammered. "Do you know where I can find a mop?"

The security officer obviously didn't speak English. We didn't speak Korean. The officer got angrier and angrier. Tomas and I gave him blank stares.

"What's the big deal?" Tomas said under his breath to me, "I'll clean it up."

The security officer blew his whistle again. Another officer ran into the exhibit room. He too looked at the buckets. Then he threw his hands up in the air. The two security officers talked loudly to one another.

"Let's get out of here." I grabbed Tomas by the hand. "Run."

We ran as fast as we could through the exhibit hall, trying to find our way out of the museum. I heard whistles blowing. I turned to look. It was the security guards, chasing us.

"You spill some water and they want to arrest you," Tomas huffed as he ran.

I could see the museum doors. If we could just get through the doors and out into the Olympic Park, we could lose the officers for sure.

Until Aunt Bernadette stepped in. She literally walked right into us. We almost knocked her over because we were running so fast.

"Whoa, kids, where are you going in such a hurry?"

Whistles blowing, the security officers barreled down the hallway, right for us.

"Uh-oh, looks like trouble," Aunt Bernadette said.

The officers ran up to us, grabbed our arms, and yelled at us in Korean. They started to drag us away from Aunt Bernadette. She reached for me, then one of the officers grabbed her arm too and led the three of us away.

"What in the world?" Aunt Bernadette said.

"I don't know. Tomas knocked over some buckets of water and these guys want to arrest us," I told her.

They took us to an office room for questioning.

Aunt Bernadette said, "American. English. Please."

The officers looked at one another. One left the room and returned with a well-dressed Korean man. Aunt Bernadette smiled at the man, like she recognized him. Then she stepped forward and gave him a kiss on the cheek. What is she doing? I thought. She's out of her mind.

The man in the suit spoke English. He was the curator of the museum.

"Bernadette Perez, I can't believe it's you, after all these years." The curator smiled and held her hand tenderly.

"Hwan! It's you," she said, smiling. "When was the last time I saw you? Five? Six years ago?"

He nodded. "You are as lovely as ever."

"Oh, thank you. And you are as handsome as ever."

Tomas looked at me and whispered, "Since when did Aunt Bernadette have a Korean boyfriend?"

I shrugged my shoulders. "Beats me."

It turns out that Aunt Bernadette and Hwan went to college together in Chicago. They dated for a few months until he decided to go home to Korea to work.

Hwan listened patiently to the angry security guards. Then he asked for Tomas's side of the story.

Tomas told him they should really fix the leaky roof. That's when Hwan laughed.

"Children, the roof is fine. Those buckets are art."

I was confused.

"You knocked over a piece of modern art. That's why the guards chased you. They thought you were vandalizing the artwork," Hwan explained.

"No, sir," Tomas said. "I didn't mean to knock art over. I swear."

Aunt Bernadette spoke up on Tomas's behalf. "Hwan, would it be okay with you if Marisol and Tomas cleaned up the mess and set up the buckets?"

"Of course, you can help. You can mop up the spilled water but I'll have to call the artist to set up her display again. So it is just right," Hwan said.

While Tomas and I mopped up buckets of water, Hwan and Aunt Bernadette sat on a nearby bench.

"They look like lovebirds," Tomas said.

"Hey, he probably saved your skin," I reminded Tomas. "Those guards were ready to kill you."

When we finished, Hwan gave Aunt Bernadette his phone number. She apologized again for the damage.

"It was all worth it, to see you again," Hwan told her.

As we walked out of the museum, we saw Mom and Dad.

"They don't need to know what happened, kids. It's over and done with," Aunt Bernadette said and winked at us.

"Were you really in love with him?" I whispered to Aunt Bernadette.

"Yes, I almost married him," she answered.

"Why didn't you?"

"I didn't want to leave my family in America." She gave me a quick squeeze.

"Are you going to call him?" I asked.

"No, no." She shook her head. "That was so long ago."

We walked out of the museum, into the bright, warm sunlight.

"I'm hungry," Tomas said. "Let's go find a Korean barbeque."

The rest of us moaned. "Oh, not again!"

I pleaded, "Please, can we try something new?"

We laughed as we walked down the street, looking for dinner. I hoped it wouldn't be Korean barbeque again.

Chapter Nine

War Memorial

It's not easy having a history professor for a parent. If there's a museum or war memorial within a hundred miles, Dad will find it.

As soon as we hopped off the subway and found the War Memorial of Korea, Tomas was overjoyed. Fighter airplanes lined the wide sidewalk.

"Planes, Mari, planes!" Tomas shouted in my ear, "TANKS! TANKS! TANKS!"

"Yes, I can see that," I said dryly.

"Come on, Marisol, Tomas behaved himself when you took us to the mall the other afternoon. Now it's his turn for fun," Mom said sternly.

"Fine," I replied. But I knew I wouldn't like it. I'm not into military history like Dad and Tomas are.

As soon as we went into the museum, Dad and Tomas ran off to see the exhibits.

"Mari, let's go with the guys," Mom said.

"No, thanks. I don't like war and stuff. I'll wait in the lobby and read a book on my phone."

"Suit yourself," Mom said. "Call me if you need anything." She went to catch up with Dad and Tomas.

I found a quiet corner and sat down to read. Just as I was settling in, a large group of Korean high school students came through the doors. They wore clean, neat uniforms and carried tablets to take notes in. The teachers wore business suits and looked serious.

"You, over there. Hello!" one young teacher said to me.

I looked up, surprised.

"Yes?"

"Where are you from?"

"Chicago," I answered.

A muffled "Ooohh" came from the group of students.

The teacher led the group closer to me. "What are you doing in Korea and not in Chicago at school?"

"I'm here with my father. He is teaching at a university."

The teacher looked concerned.

"I'm home schooled," I said. "My parents teach me at home."

The Korean teacher did not look happy.

"We take education very seriously in Korea," the teacher said. "Everyone goes to school."

I nodded. "Yes, we do too."

One Korean girl asked, "Why are you sitting here all by yourself?"

"Well, I, uh, I didn't really want to go into the museum." I realized that seemed like a weak reason.

"You can learn so much from this museum, so much history," a boy said.

The teacher spoke up. "How do you expect to get into a good college if you don't study and learn?"

"I do learn. All the time," I said defensively.

The teacher narrowed her eyes at me. "But you don't want to go into the museum to learn?"

I must seem like a horrible student, I thought. *But I'm not!*

"Come with us. You can't sit here in a corner all day," the teacher commanded. I joined their field trip. I didn't want to look like a dumb American.

The tour guide led us through the exhibit. We saw every type of bullet ever made. As we walked, a girl, Nari, asked me about America.

"Will you go to college?"Nari asked.

"Oh sure, but I'm only twelve. I have about six years until I need to worry about college."

Nari looked shocked. "What if you don't get into the best college?"

I shrugged. "I guess I'll apply to another one."

Nari seemed terrified at this plan of mine.

"What's the big deal?" I asked Nari.

"In Korea, you must be the best to get into college. I go to school from eight a.m. to four p.m. Then I go to a hagwon from six p.m. to nine p.m., for extra studying."

"Monday through Friday?" I asked.

Nari nodded. "And two Saturdays every month."

"You're never home," I said.

"I have to be the best. Everyone does. We all need well-paying jobs after college."

I knew some competitive people but I'd never met anyone quite so dedicated to school. Sure, I enjoyed homeschooling. I knew I wanted to go to college. But I never studied for twelve or thirteen hours a day.

"Maybe someday Korea will be the most powerful nation in the world," Nari said, only half-jokingly.

What about America? I thought but didn't say out loud. I better study a little harder.

Our group met up with my family near the war uniform exhibit. Mom looked happy that I'd made some new friends. I introduced the group to them. I think the teacher looked more comfortable after meeting my parents. Like maybe I wasn't such a slacker after all.

We said our goodbyes and thanked them for letting me tag along with them. As we walked away, Dad said, "That sure was nice of them to include you, Marisol."

Mom added, "They were a sweet group of kids."

"Yeah, but they thought I was a loser because I'm homeschooled and I don't go to a hagwon in the evenings to learn more."

Mom and Dad chuckled. "We can arrange that," Mom joked.

"Koreans are known for their hard work in school. That's why their country is doing so well. They take education seriously," Dad said.

"Mari," Mom said, rubbing my back, "don't worry, honey. You'll do fine. You'll get into college. No problem."

After talking to the Korean teacher and Nari, I didn't believe Mom anymore.

"Sweetheart, you're only a sixth grader. Relax and enjoy your childhood," Mom said.

With that, Tomas let out a loud burp that echoed across the courtyard.

"How's that for awesome?" He giggled. "Korean soda pop gives me gas."

I couldn't help but laugh at Tomas. He always knew how to make me feel better.

Chapter Ten

The Palace

I have to admit it: I love, love, love all things related to royalty. Kings, queens, princes, castles – I daydream about them all the time. I wonder what it would be like to be royalty, to live in a palace, to have beautiful gowns, and to give fancy parties. When Mom suggested we visit Changgyeonggung Palace, in the heart of Seoul, she didn't have to ask me twice. I was ready to go see the palace. Even Tomas thought it would be cool. He liked stories about terrifying dragons and heroic knights.

Changgyeonggung Palace is a large, walled-off palace surrounded by modern high rise buildings and busy highways. I can only imagine what it would have been like five or six hundred years ago, without the tall buildings and traffic.

We walked through three massive gates. Tomas said there were three gates to stop people from breaking through and killing the king. Inside the palace, graceful buildings surrounded a stone courtyard and pond.

"This palace was built for queens," Mom told us. But the king also had visitors to the palace, too.

"When the Japanese invaded Korea in 1592, many of the original palace buildings were destroyed," Mom read from a nearby sign.

"These are not the real buildings?" Tomas asked.

"They're built to look exactly like the original buildings," Mom answered.

Tomas looked a little disappointed.

"Tomi," I said, "A lot can happen in five hundred years. You should be glad they even remember or know what the original buildings looked like."

"I guess so," he said rather sadly.

"Let's go see Tongmyeongjeon," Mom suggested. "The king and queen lived there."

Tongmyeongjeon is a hall. But don't let that fool you. The roof reminded me of a boat or sailing ship, deep and beautiful. As we walked through Tongmyeongjeon, Mom read us a story about the king and a woman. King Sukjong kept a woman in Tongmyeongjeon. He was very much in love with this woman. But, this woman, Jang Hui-Bin, wanted to curse Queen Inhyeon. So Jang Hui-Bin buried dead animals and puppets in the front of Tongmyeongjeon to fulfill the curse against the queen.

"That's pretty creepy," I said quietly.

"Do you think the curse worked?" Tomas asked me.

"Kids," Mom interrupted us, "I need to find a bathroom. Wait here for me. I'll be right back."

Tomas and I walked around the hall again. I snapped a few more photos, especially of the large sweeping roof. Tomas sat down on a stone step to wait for Mom. He lazily kicked a few stones around.

A stone came loose from the floor of the courtyard.

"Tomi," I snapped at him. "Don't break it."

"I didn't. This stone came loose."

He didn't look worried. In fact, he dug the toe of his shoe deeper into the sand that was under the stone.

"Oh my goodness, Mari!" Tomas squealed. "I found bones!"

I stopped taking pictures of the hall and rushed over to him. By his toes there were small, frail bones.

"What did they belong to?" Tomas asked.

I bent down to take a closer look. "A bird. See the wings?"

"We found the curse," Tomas said a little amazed.

"I hope we're not cursed now because of it," I tried to joke. But actually, I'm kind of superstitious. I won't step on cracks in the sidewalk because I'm afraid I'll break my mother's back. I never walk under ladders. And, if I see a black cat crossing the street in front of me, I'll turn and go the other way so it doesn't cross my path. What if we did renew the curse?

"Hi kids," Mom called as she walked up to us. "What are you looking at?"

Tomas pointed to the ground. "We found bones," he said.

"Interesting," Mom said thoughtfully. "Small, delicate bird bones. Possibly a canary or finch. Once a royal pet." Our mom is a world-famous bird biologist. She knows her bird bones.

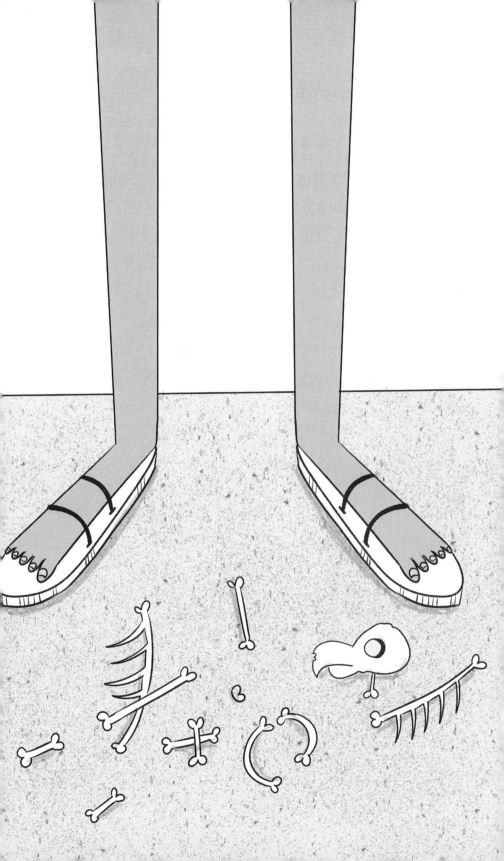

Mom looked up from the bones. "Why are you two so pale? You've seen animal bones before."

It was true. Mom had bones in her office at the college. She had bone collections in the museum. She even had boxes of bones in our dining room in Chicago. But the bones in the palace courtyard were different. These bones were part of a curse.

"You better put the stone back in place," I told Tomas. "Don't want to get into trouble."

Tomas moved the stone over the bird bones.

"Maybe if it is put back, we won't be cursed," he said hopefully.

Chapter Eleven

The Curse

And that was our fabulous adventure in Korea, before we were captured by the North Korean military.

We'd been waiting for five hours now. No news from Mom and Dad. No news from the North Korean government. Just waiting, waiting, and more waiting.

Tomas whispered to me, "I bet this is part of the curse. Remember the bird bones we found in the palace?"

Of course I remembered. That very thought had been nagging at me for the last couple of hours.

If we awakened the ancient curse at the palace, then what would happen to us? We'd be doomed for sure. We might die in a prison cell in North Korea, never to see our parents again.

"Aunt Bernadette," I said softly. "Do you believe in curses?"

She looked surprised. "Why do you ask, honey?"

I explained what had happened at the palace in Seoul with the bird bones.

"That's a creepy story," she agreed. "But I don't believe in curses."

"You don't?" Tomas looked skeptical.

"Nope. I believe that you make your own luck. You map your own destiny," she said triumphantly.

"Then explain how all this happened," I questioned her. I still believed the curse was at work here.

"Honey," Aunt Bernadette said, "bad things happen to good people all the time. You've just got to learn how to deal with it and bounce back."

"What are those North Koreans going to do to us?" Tomas asked. His voice trembled.

Aunt Bernadette shrugged. "Tomi, I honestly don't know. I hope they'll at least let me make a phone call to your mom and dad."

A severe-looking military officer marched into the room.

"Bernadette Perez," he barked.

"Yes, sir," Aunt Bernadette answered.

"You are in serious trouble. You and these two

children have crossed into unfriendly land. We in the north have been at war with South Korea for over sixty years," he said gruffly.

Aunt Bernadette nodded her head. She looked calmly at the officer, waiting for him to continue his speech.

"We have searched your background. We found information that made us suspicious."

Aunt Bernadette took a big gulp to clear her throat. I noticed small beads of sweat glisten on her forehead. She was getting nervous.

"You dated a South Korean man while you were in college. You went to anti-war protests as a college student. You have had three speeding tickets. You and these children ran into some trouble at the War Memorial." The officer paused for a second and continued to read from his tablet.

"This girl," he pointed at me, "has been seen with a dangerous South Korean K-Pop star, possibly even dated him. We don't like pop stars in North Korea." The officer gave me a dark, sinister stare.

Now it was my turn to get nervous. Even though I didn't really date TaeYang, the TV stations sure made it look like I was his new love interest. I started to defend myself.

"Hush, stupid child. We have data. We know what you did," he barked.

Aunt Bernadette motioned for me to remain silent. The officer continued. "The father of these children teaches at an American university. Now he is in South Korea, possibly spreading anti-North Korea information to hundreds of young people. You are a very dangerous family," he said.

I never thought of my family as dangerous. Silly, quirky, unusual maybe, but never dangerous.

"You will wait here. We must consult the lieutenant to see what must be done with the three of you." With that, the officer turned and marched from the room, locking the steel door behind him.

Tomas started to whimper again.

"Shh, hush," Aunt Bernadette said, patting my brother on the back. "We're not dangerous. Foolish maybe but not dangerous. They'll figure it all out soon and let us go back to South Korea."

Aunt Bernadette tried to put on a brave face but I could tell by the worried creases on her forehead and the sweat on her brow that maybe, just maybe we were actually cursed.

Several hours passed. We hadn't eaten anything since breakfast. My stomach ached. I could hear Tomas's grumbling. Aunt Bernadette looked tired. The steel door clicked open.

In walked Aunt Bernadette's old boyfriend, Hwan. Aunt Bernadette looked stunned to say the least. Hwan was all business-like. He didn't move to even shake Aunt Bernadette's hand let alone kiss her.

"Ms. Perez," Hwan said to Aunt Bernadette, "You have violated very serious international laws. North Korea could retain you for the rest of your life."

Aunt Bernadette shifted nervously on her feet.

"But I have worked out a deal with the North Korean officials. They are to let you and the children go free if you promise to never go near the demilitarized zone again," Hwan said seriously.

Aunt Bernadette nodded her head, "Yes, yes, of course. I promise."

"Perfect," Hwan replied. Then he looked at Tomas and I. "Children, you must start to wake up and pay attention. What you did by canoeing through the inlet could have cost you your lives."

I was horribly ashamed. Hwan was right. What Tomas and I did was foolish. What were we thinking? The problem was, we weren't thinking.

"You are not home in comfortable America. You are visiting a country that has been at war for over sixty years. This border is the most heavily armed and heavily patrolled border in the entire world. It is no laughing matter."

"Yes sir," we whispered as we stared at the floor.

Hwan went on. "Obviously, the two of you paid absolutely no attention to anything you learned while you traveled through South Korea. If you had, you would have known to stay out of the inlet."

Hwan paused. "Nevertheless," he added, "I've managed to convince the North Korean government that the three of you are simply foolish American tourists who pose no threat to their national security."

As soon as Hwan said that, Aunt Bernadette rushed to him and threw her arms around him. He blushed a little and then pried her arms off of himself.

"The officers will let you come with me. I will

take you back across the border into South Korea."

Aunt Bernadette, overjoyed, clapped her hands together. She exclaimed, "Oh, Hwan, thank you, thank you."

The officer returned to the room. Hwan signed paperwork. Aunt Bernadette signed paperwork. By midnight, we were in a private car, crossing the border back into South Korea.

Hwan drove us to our apartment. Before Aunt Bernadette left Hwan, she asked him, "What can I do to repay this favor?"

"You can go on a date with me." He smiled.

Aunt Bernadette giggled like a teenager. "How could I possibly tell you no after all this? You saved us from North Korea!"

She gave Hwan a peck on the cheek. "Stop by tomorrow, for dinner," she said.

He smiled and wished us goodnight.

Once we got inside our apartment, Mom and Dad rushed to us, covering us with hugs and kisses.

"Oh, we thought we'd never see you again," Mom cried.

"Hwan is a hero," Dad gushed. "If it wasn't for him, you'd still be in North Korea."

Aunt Bernadette looked thoughtfully, and asked Dad, "What do you mean exactly?"

Dad, surprised at what he let slip out of his mouth, tried to cover it up. "Um, nothing. Don't worry about it."

"Alberto," Aunt Bernadette said sternly. "Confess. You know you can't hide anything from your big sister."

"Fine. But all of you must promise to never breathe a word of this to anyone."

We all agreed.

"Hwan has worked as a spy for South Korea since returning from college. He knew the minute the North Korean government captured you guys." Dad smiled. He was pretty proud of his secret information.

I shook my head. "No, he's a curator at the museum," I said.

"That's one of his covers," Dad explained. "He's really a spy. It was just luck that he ran into you at the museum."

Aunt Bernadette was almost speechless for a change. "I don't believe it. My dear, sweet Hwan is a spy. Who would have guessed?"

Dad laughed. "Gee, Bernadette, doesn't this sound like something out of a Hollywood movie?"

She gave Dad an amused smirk. "Oh boy, does it. And, to make it even crazier, I promised I'd go out to dinner with him, for helping us out of North Korea. A real date."

Chapter Twelve

Lovebirds

Aunt Bernadette was true to her word. She went out to dinner with Hwan the night after he freed us from North Korea.

In fact, the date went so well, for the next two months, they went out almost every day.

"Bernadette, you look like you're in love," Mom remarked one morning at breakfast.

Aunt Bernadette blushed. "I think I am. At my age, it is silly," she giggled.

"It is never too late for love," Mom said.

"See kids," Aunt Bernadette said to me and Tomas, "It wasn't some ancient curse that got us into North Korea."

"What was it then?" Tomas asked sarcastically.

"I'd say it was magic," Aunt Bernadette said dreamily.

"Ugh," Tomas groaned. "She's lovesick. She

doesn't know what she's talking about."

Mom and Aunt Bernadette laughed at Tomas.

"So you don't believe in curses. But you do believe in magic. Where do you draw the line? What's the difference between the two?" Tomas asked.

"Oh, Tomas, I believe in good things, in good magic. I try to find the silver lining in every cloud. I don't go around looking for bad things. That's no way to live your life," Aunt Bernadette answered.

"But you're dating a spy, someone who goes around looking for bad things," I said.

"Oh no, he doesn't look for bad things. He looks for things that might save lives or help people."

"Whatever," I said. "He's still a spy."

We only had one month left in Korea. Dad's teaching job at the university was almost over. Then we'd head home to Chicago for the rest of the summer. Although we enjoyed Seoul, we were tired of bumping into each other in our tiny apartment. We needed our own bedrooms. I actually couldn't wait to get home and use our dishwasher after scrubbing dishes in the tiny sink every night. Yuck.

"Will you stay in Korea?" Mom quietly asked

Aunt Bernadette. I think Mom hoped I wouldn't hear that question, although it was hard not to when the kitchen was only three feet wide.

"I don't know, Carolina. I haven't felt this way about anyone in a long time," Aunt Bernadette answered thoughtfully.

The next evening, after Aunt Bernadette came back from her date with Hwan, she brought Hwan upstairs to our apartment.

They looked serious. Hwan said he needed to speak to Dad. I was afraid North Korea was watching us again, or waiting to capture us.

"Mr. Perez, Alberto," Hwan said respectfully. "I am very much in love with your sister. With your permission, I would like to marry her."

Dad almost spit out the coffee he was drinking.

"Marry Bernadette?" Dad sputtered.

Bernadette and Hwan nodded.

"Bernadette, have you thought about this? Where will you live?" Dad asked her.

"Alberto, don't worry. I am a grown up. I can handle this."

"Yes, I know that. But he's a spy," Dad said and then quickly added, "No offense, Hwan."

"Yes, I am aware of that, Alberto. We have it all planned out. After the wedding, we'll go back to Chicago. Hwan will make Chicago his home when he's not needed in South Korea."

"Sounds like a lot of work," Dad said.

"It might be, but we love each other," Aunt Bernadette said.

"Alberto, I will take good care of Bernadette. I love her," Hwan said. "We'd like your approval."

"Yes! Yes!" Mom said. Dad shot her an angry look but gave in.

The grown-ups hugged. Mom congratulated them.

"When's the wedding?" I asked.

"Next week," answered Aunt Bernadette. "Friday."

This time Dad did spit out his coffee.

For the next week, we saw little of Hwan. Aunt Bernadette dragged us from market to market, trying to find fresh flowers for the wedding. She went to a Korean bridal shop and found a simple white dress to wear.

"I'd never thought I'd be a bride," Aunt Bernadette said, sighing.

With all of the details taken care of, on Friday, Aunt Bernadette stood by the Olympic Lake, waiting to marry Hwan. She looked beautiful in her simple white gown. Mom, Dad, Tomas, and I were dressed in our finest clothes.

Hwan was ten minutes late.

"Oh, he's probably stuck in traffic," Mom reassured Aunt Bernadette.

Ten more minutes passed.

Mom said one word to Aunt Bernadette. "Traffic."

Ten more minutes passed.

"Still traffic," Mom said.

After an hour passed and there was no sign of Hwan, Aunt Bernadette started to cry. "I'm so foolish. To think Hwan wanted to marry me, me, after all these years."

Mom handed Aunt Bernadette tissues. "There, there," Mom tried to sound positive. "I'm sure there's a logical reason why Hwan is not here."

A messenger ran to us by the fountain. He handed Dad a message.

"Dear Alberto, please tell Bernadette that I love her very much. But an emergency has come up at the border. As soon as I return, I will find her and we will be married."

Dad shook his head in disbelief.

"I guess stuff like that happens when you fall in love with a spy," Tomas said.

I hugged Aunt Bernadette. "He'll come back for you," I whispered to her. She nodded but tears splashed down her cheeks.

We rode the subway back to our apartment. It was a quiet, awkward ride. No one knew what to say to Aunt Bernadette to make her feel better.

"Maybe it was the curse after all," Tomas said quietly to me as we were getting ready for bed.

"Shh, Tomi, now is not the time to talk about curses. Aunt Bernadette is sad enough," I said.

The day before we were to leave for Chicago, Hwan showed up at our apartment. He looked thinner than before and slightly worried.

He spoke with Aunt Bernadette in the kitchen. Afterword, Hwan left and Aunt Bernadette came to talk with the family.

"Hwan is so sorry," Aunt Bernadette told us. "It was an emergency and South Korea needed him right away."

"Do you forgive him?" Mom asked Aunt Bernadette.

"I do," she said. "I forgive him. But I don't like him disappearing without a word. I realized I can't marry a spy. I need to know where my husband is."

"What will you do?" I asked.

"I'll head home to Chicago and wait for magic to find me," she smiled.

That's exactly what she did. Three months later, Hwan appeared at Aunt Bernadette's Chicago apartment with a huge bouquet of flowers.

"I'm retired now. No more spying for me. Will you marry me?" he asked Aunt Bernadette as he bent down on one knee.

She grabbed him and exclaimed, "Oh, you silly man, yes! Yes!"

The magic found her. She was right after all. There's no such thing as curses.

Marisol's Travel Journal

One of my favorite Korean foods: Pajeon

Pajeon Recipe
(Savory Green Onion Pancake)

Ingredients
Batter:
1 cup flour
1 teaspoon salt
1 cup cold water

Filling:
a bunch of green onions (end stems cut off)
1 egg (beaten)
1 sliced red pepper
Dipping Sauce:
1/4 cup soy sauce
1 tablespoon rice wine vinegar
1 clove minced garlic
1 teaspoon sesame oil
1 diced red pepper

Directions
Take all the dipping sauce ingredients and pour them into a small bowl. Let them set for 20 minutes.

Place the flour and salt in a large mixing bowl. Whisk in cold water to prevent it from getting lumpy.

Beat one egg and set it aside.

Wash the green onions. Cut off any parts of the stems that are too tough.

Get a frying pan ready. Put it on medium heat and add oil for frying. Swirl the oil to coat the pan. NOTE: Use a pan big enough to match the full length of the onions.

Once the frying pan is hot, place your green onions into the batter and coat them. Try to keep them in as straight a line as possible. Keep them flat.

Using tongs or long cooking chopsticks, quickly and gently place the battered green onions into the hot pan. Try to lay them out as flat and evenly as possible. Quickly take the remaining batter and fill in any gaps between the onions to join them into one solid pancake. Use your spatula to shape the pancake.

Watch the surface of the pancake. After a minute or two it will become solid with little bubbles starting to pop. Pour the beaten egg evenly all over the pancake. Use the spatula to keep the egg from spilling out onto the pan, and fold it back onto the pancake.

After another one or two minutes the egg will become more solid. Use the spatula to lift the pancake. Be careful that the bottom is not burned. It should be lightly browned. Flip it when it is lightly browned. Let it cook for another two to three minutes on this side. Be sure to check the bottom again so it doesn't burn.

Serve the pancake by slicing it into a grid shape and serve with the dipping sauce.

Country Facts

Republic of Korea (South Korea)

Capital: Seoul

Official Language: Korean, Hangeul

Population: 51 million

Climate: Cold, dry winters and humid, hot summers

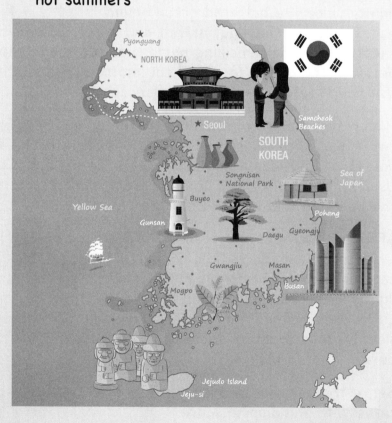

Famous people
Queen Sondok (first female ruler of
    Korea, 632-647 CE)
King Sejong (ruler, 1397-1450)
Son Yeon Jae (Olympic rhythmic gymnast)

Significant Events
1945: End of World War II, Korea divided by the
38th parallel, making it two nations
1953: End of Korean War, demilitarized zone
created
1988: Seoul, Korea, hosted Olympic Games

Events and Holidays
February: Seoul Holiday
May 5: Children's Day
May 8: Parents Day
May 25: Buddha's Birthday
June 6: Memorial Day
September: Mid-Autumn Festival
October 3: National Foundation Day
October 9: Hangeul Proclamation Day
December 25: Christmas

Landmarks

Beomeosa Temple, where we saw a fighting monk!

Jeju Island, Hallasan, the ancient volcano

Jagalchi Fish Market (Not a pet store, Tomas!)

Olympic Park and the World Peace Gate

War Memorial of Korea

Now and Then

Korea is an ancient empire. It was once conquered by the Japanese. Today, Japan no longer controls Korea but North and South Korea are divided. South Korea has a growing, powerful economy with high rates of education. North Korea does not have freedom and struggles to keep up with the rest of the world.

Changgyeonggung Palace is a temple built for queens 500 years ago. Today it is popular with tourists.

Discussion Questions

1. Describe the history of Korea. Why did the country split into North and South Korea?

2. Name the historic sites that Marisol and Tomas experienced. What did they find at these places? Describe what they thought of these places.

3. Marisol and Tomas learned about K-Pop music. How is it alike and/or different from American pop music?

4. Marisol and Tomas learned about fresh fish markets. How is a Korean fish market alike or different from an American grocery store?

5. Explain the typical day of a Korean high school student. Why is their school day so long?

6. Tomas and Marisol are homeschooled. How might their school day be different than the average Korean student?

7. How did the 1988 Olympics change the city of Seoul? What did Seoul want to show to the rest of the world?

Vocabulary

Did you know what each of these words meant in the story? Try using them in your own story about a visit to Korea.

communist

demilitarized zone

democracy

government

K-pop

military

modern art

Olympic Games

peace

royalty

spy

superstitious

Websites to Visit

www.timeforkids.com/destination/south-korea

www.kids.nationalgeographic.com/content/kids/en_US/
explore/countries/south-korea

www.scholastic.com/teachers/article/south-korea

About the Author

Precious McKenzie lives in Montana and teaches writing to college students. She loves to help her college students become stronger writers. When she is not helping her students, Precious enjoys using her imagination to tell funny stories in books for children.

About the Illustrator

Becka Moore studied Illustration for Children's Publishing in the North of Wales at Glyndwr University. She has since moved back home to Manchester where she works under the strict supervision of two very mischievous cats, doodling away and drinking far too much coffee.